Policeman Lou and Policewoman Sue

by Lisa Desimini

THE BLUE SKY PRESS

AN IMPRINT OF SCHOLASTIC INC. • NEW YORK

THE BLUE SKY PRESS

Copyright © 2003 by Lisa Desimini

For information regarding permission, please write to: Permissions Department, Scholastic Inc., 557 Broadway, New York, New York 10012.

SCHOLASTIC, THE BLUE SKY PRESS, and associated logos are trademarks and/or registered trademarks of Scholastic Inc.

Library of Congress catalog card number: 2002006041

ISBN 0-439-40888-1

10 9 8 7 6 5 4 3 2   03 04 05 06 07

Printed in Singapore   46

First printing, June 2003

Designed by Kathleen Westray

SPECIAL THANKS TO

Scott Michaels, Michelle Woods,
Estelle Von Alt, Matt Mahurin,
Bonnie Verburg, and
Robert Martin Staenberg

FOR THE MURPHY FAMILY—
Anna, Katherine, Sean, and
Anthony, Chief of Police
at Rutgers University

Policeman Lou and
Policewoman Sue have
a cup of coffee and a muffin
together every morning.
Then their day begins.

Policeman Lou walks down the street saying hello
to everyone. Rocky the florist is watering his plants,
and Jessie the baker is putting out this morning's buns.
Policeman Lou makes sure everything is okay.

Policewoman Sue holds up her hand,
and all the cars STOP.
Now, the twins, Tommy and Tim,
can cross the street and go to school.

There's a stray dog.
"Come here, Poochie," say Policeman Lou
and Policewoman Sue. They take him back
to the station and give him some water.

Then they check his tag. His name is Rags.
Everyone at the station will be sad
to see Rags go when his owner
comes to pick him up.

Later, Policeman Lou and Policewoman Sue see that a car is parked in front of a fire hydrant.

"They must have been in a rush," says Sue.

"Must not be from around here," says Lou. "There would be no place for the fire truck to park."

"It's not safe," says Sue.

Sue writes a ticket for thirty dollars
and leaves it on the windshield of the car.

It's time for lunch.
Policewoman Sue and Policeman Lou hop into

their police car and go to the diner
for grilled cheese sandwiches and iced tea.

Polly, behind the counter, asks about their day.

"It's been a good day," says Policeman Lou.

"Yes, it's been a quiet day," says Policewoman Sue.

Lunch Specials

grilled cheese on Rye
macaroni-n-cheese
Roast beef on whole wheat
Fruit Salad with cottage cheese
Polly's homemade chocolate cake

Suddenly, a worried crowd
is gathering outside.

Sue and Lou jump up to see what's going on. A woman's purse has been stolen.

Policewoman Sue asks the woman if she's okay and writes a police report.

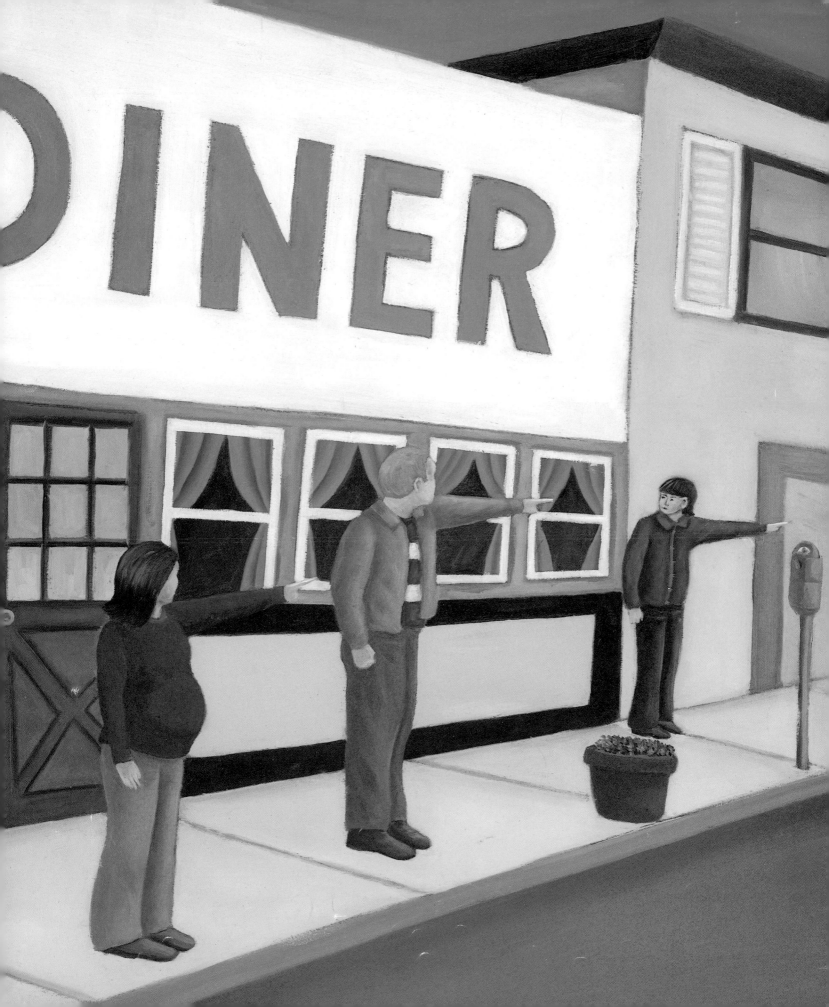

Policeman Lou blows his whistle and
runs down the street after the robber.
The woman says, "Yes, that's him!"

Policeman Lou catches him, puts the handcuffs on him, and says, "You're under arrest." Then he reads the man his rights.

Then Policeman Lou, Policewoman Sue, and the arrested man ride in the police car down to the station. The woman's purse is photographed for evidence.

The robber gets fingerprinted and photographed,
and he gets to make *one* phone call.
Then they put him in the jail cell.

Policeman Lou and
Policewoman Sue
look at each other.

"Our job is
never boring,"
they both say.

The woman gets her purse back.
"Thank you," she says.
"My grocery money and my favorite picture
of my grandson are in here."

Policeman Lou and Policewoman Sue write up
a crime incident report and give it to their sergeant.
"It's time to call it a day," says Policeman Lou.
"Well done," says Policewoman Sue.

Policewoman Sue invites Policeman Lou over for dinner and makes his favorite meal—chicken and peas and mashed potatoes, with peach pie for dessert.

Then Lou washes and Sue dries.

"Good-night Sue," says Lou.
"Good-night Lou," says Sue. "See you in the morning."
"Let's hope it's a quiet day tomorrow," they both say.

Policeman Lou and Policewoman Sue's Ten Favorite Safety Tips for Children

1. Never talk to strangers.

2. If a stranger asks you questions, offers you candy or gifts, or asks you to go near his/her car or home, do not go, and do not answer. Run home and tell a trusted adult as fast as you can.

3. Be careful crossing streets—always look both ways. Only cross the street with an adult's permission.

4. Don't play with matches, lighters, or other things that might start a fire.

5. Obey traffic laws and signs when bike riding, and always wear a helmet.

6. Respect the rights and property of others.

7. Remember to keep doors and windows locked if you are home alone.

8. Keep the police station emergency phone number, often 911, next to your family phone.

9. Guns are not toys. If you find a gun, tell an adult, or call 911.

10. When you need help, talk to a trusted adult or a friend.

• What other safety tips do you know?

• Policemen and policewomen do hundreds of tasks in small towns and big cities everywhere. Can you think of some things they do in your community?